THE GATEWAY

THE FOUR-FINGERED MAN

Cerberus Jones

Kane Miller
A DIVISION OF EDC PUBLISHING

First American Edition 2016
Kane Miller, A Division of EDC Publishing

Text copyright © 2015 Chris Morphew, Rowan McAuley and David Harding
Illustration and design copyright © 2015 Hardie Grant Egmont
First published in Australia by Hardie Grant Egmont 2015

For information contact:
Kane Miller, A Division of EDC Publishing
P.O. Box 470663
Tulsa, OK 74147-0663
www.kanemiller.com
www.edcpub.com
www.usbornebooksandmore.com

Library of Congress Control Number: 2015954192

Printed and bound in the United States of America
7 8 9 10

ISBN: 978-1-61067-498-0

PROLOGUE

In the last moments before dawn, a man in a black trench coat slipped out from the shadow of the old hotel. The grass was wet against his legs and the silence around him was broken only by the distant crash of waves against the cliffs below.

He hurried.

If anyone was watching, they would have noticed how heavily his coat sat across his shoulders, how his back stooped under the weight, and how the bulging pockets bumped against his legs with every step. They may even have seen when – unnoticed by him – a small glinting object and a flurry of eucalyptus leaves fell from the man's pocket and landed in the long grass.

But no one was watching. Not even the sound of birds broke the spell as he stepped into a grove of ancient magnolia trees and disappeared into their shadows.

He was a tall man, but so thin and angular the leaves hardly crackled under his feet. As he walked, his hands kept straying to his pockets, patting them gently as though reassuring himself that his cargo was still safe.

Hidden in a clearing beyond the magnolias was an old tin-roofed cottage – so run-down and shabby it was really more of a shack. The man slowed, looking around carefully, before stepping out from the trees and striding towards the cottage.

Before his hand reached the door it swung open from inside, and a scowling face with a mess of gray hair appeared through the gap. "Where have you been?"

The man in the coat hurried inside, brushing past the gray-haired man, who locked and bolted the door behind them.

"You're late," the gray-haired man grumbled.

"Nonsense. My connection shall arrive momentarily."

"It *should* have arrived already. According to my charts –"

"Your charts are wrong, Tom," said the man in the coat. "And they're only going to get worse. I, on the other hand –"

He paused as a deep shudder ran through the cottage, rattling the windows.

"– am right on time."

Tom opened his mouth and closed it again,

3

a look of frustration passing over his face. The cottage shuddered a second time, and a deep groan came from the far room. Or not *from* the room: somehow, the sound came from under it.

Tom's eyes narrowed. "Show-off." Then he held out a weathered hand. "Give it to me."

The man in the coat nodded and put a hand to his throat. No, not to his throat – somehow he slid the tips of his fingers *into* his throat and felt around inside his own neck. There was a clicking sound, a fizz, and the man's face flickered as he delicately plucked a small black-and-bronze cylinder out of his neck.

The moment he dropped it into Tom's hand – the moment his own fingers lost contact with the object – the man in the coat was no longer a man. He still wore the trench coat but his pale skin and black hair had vanished, replaced by the glittering, metallic-blue shell of an insect.

His long white fingers had become the curved black hooks of a beetle, and iridescent wings twitched beneath his coat.

Tom scowled at him, and then at the device in his hand. "Hey! This isn't mine! Where's the one I gave you?"

The insect patted at its coat pockets and chittered, clattering its mandibles.

"Fine, fine, you don't have time to worry about that. You don't have to convince *me* that the Krskn issue is more important. But you do realize the new owners arrive today? Last thing I need is for them to find any clues that you've been here."

The insect started to move towards the other room, picking its way through a bizarre clutter of broken cuckoo clocks, windup toys and stacks of leather-bound books.

A gust of hot air swept through the cottage, and that terrible, abysmal groan sounded again.

"It's here!" said Tom. "Go on! Not that you've ever been bothered to wait for a connection before ..." he added in a mutter.

The insect buzzed harshly.

"No, I'm *not* asking any questions. Just go!"

The room beyond the doorway was empty. Bare floorboards amplified the noise of the insect's feet as it scuttled over to the hole in the far corner of the room. That hot, rank wind blew again, gusting up the stone steps that disappeared into the darkness beneath the cottage floor. Then, as though giant lungs were hidden down there somewhere, the wind turned and sucked back down the stairwell.

Tom was still standing in the other room, clinging so tightly to the edge of his desk that his knuckles were white. The knuckles he had, anyway – one of his fingers was missing, a shiny patch of scar tissue in the gap.

The insect gathered up its coat, and scurried down the steps.

There was the sound of a door opening, a stronger smell of sour air and then a flash of light, and the door banged closed.

Tom sagged against his desk in relief. "Gone!"

CHAPTER ONE

It was Dad jerking on the hand brake that woke Amelia up. Her forehead bumped against the car window, and she suddenly realized three things: her neck was stiff, her mouth tasted like plastic and they were *there*.

Great.

She peeled long strands of red hair off her cheeks where she'd slept on them, and undid her seat belt.

Dad was already out of the car, bouncing along the gravel driveway in the thin gray light of the extreme early morning. It was chilly, grim and silent, but Dad flung his arms out in delight like he wanted to give the place a hug. Like he hadn't just driven all through the night to get here. Like he didn't have two kids in the back of the car who wished he'd just get back in and drive them straight home again.

"Come on, guys!" Dad beamed back at them. "Isn't this fantastic?"

James unfolded himself from the car, his long legs getting tangled in all the chip bags, headphone cords, plastic bags, sweaters and blankets in the backseat with them.

"Fantastic," James muttered. "Fantastically old. Fantastically ugly ..."

Mum ignored him, and got out of the front passenger seat, but Amelia thought he had a point.

When their parents had told Amelia and James

they were going to leave the city and move out to live in a big hotel by the sea, in a little country town nobody had ever heard of before, it had sounded ...

"Fantastically mental," James grumbled on.

But Dad was sure it would be a huge adventure.

"Just imagine," he'd said. "Mum and I will both be working from home – we'll get to be with you guys all the time. No more after-school programs. No more vacation day camp. And we'll have so much *space!* Acres of lawn and gardens and bush, and right next to the beach! In fact ..."

Here Dad looked at Amelia and said those magic words that had convinced her it would all be worth it. Worth changing schools, leaving friends and giving up gymnastics. Worth selling the apartment where she'd lived ever since she was born, with neighbors she'd known her whole life.

"Amelia, there will be so much space, you'll be able to get a puppy."

"Once we're settled in," Mum had added quickly.

Now that they were here, though, Amelia wasn't sure a puppy would be enough. Maybe not even eight puppies would be worth *this*.

The hotel was a huge, old-fashioned white building, with vine-covered pillars and a roof edged with iron lace over the grand entrance. It was built on the end of a headland, and seemed to be floating in the sky. All around was the sound of the sea, waves exploding on the rocks far, far below. Tall cliffs fell away on all sides, and maybe it *could* have been kind of lovely, but somehow the whole place felt wrong to Amelia.

Obviously, she wasn't some silly, superstitious little kid who believed in ghosts or any of that nonsense but ... if ever ghosts *did* exist, this was exactly the sort of place they would be.

Amelia looked around her, trying to ignore the chill prickling over her skin. The hotel must have once been beautiful, but now it was a mass of peeling paint, cracked windowpanes, spiderwebs and abandoned wasps' nests.

The grounds were huge and badly overgrown. The garden beds were so shaggy, they almost merged with the thick bushland beyond them. There was nothing except the long driveway she was standing on to connect them with the rest of the world.

In this case, the rest of the world meant a tiny beach town called Forgotten Bay.

"Well." Mum put her hands on her hips. "We've certainly got our work cut out for us."

"Right," said James, sarcastic as ever. "Home, sweet home. How do we get in?"

"Um," said Dad. "I thought the caretaker was going to be here to meet us ..."

"The *caretaker*?" said James. "This place has a *caretaker*?" He looked around at the missing floorboards in the wide veranda that circled the hotel. He looked at the possum poop lying all over the old swing seat, and made a face of fake admiration. "Wow. Lucky us. Imagine what a dump this place would be without someone taking *care* of it."

Amelia wished he'd shut up. But he was right. The hotel was a mess. Nothing like the neat, friendly apartment they'd had to sell back in the city.

Dad pulled out his phone and grinned as though he hadn't heard James at all. "I'll call Tom now. Let him know we're here."

James kicked at the gravel, and Amelia watched him, biting her lip.

It had been like this for a couple of months now: James being all rude and angry, and even more sarcastic than usual, and Dad just letting it glide past him without saying a word. Sometimes

Amelia caught Dad shooting a look at Mum, and once she heard Mum say, "That's enough, James," in a voice so quiet and cool that she knew Mum was furious. But apart from those clues ... what *had* gone on at James's school? No one would tell her. She had figured out that James *wasn't* expelled, and *wasn't* in trouble with the police, and you would have thought that was a good thing.

You would have also thought that if James had just escaped trouble, he would have been a bit less keen to keep looking for it, but no – ever since Whatever It Was happened, James had been acting like he wanted to start a fight with the whole world.

"You OK, cookie?" Mum put an arm around her.

Amelia really wasn't. She felt empty and miserable, but there wasn't much point saying so. She just nodded, and let Mum wrap her up in a hug.

"No reception!" Dad said, shaking his phone and finally sounding less than a thousand percent excited.

"Ha!" a voice barked out so suddenly, and so close behind them, that Amelia jumped. "You won't get any reception around here!"

An old man in a tatty, checked shirt was limping across the grass towards them. A black patch covered one of his eyes, and an ancient black cap with the words "Forgotten Bay" embroidered on the front was pulled low on his forehead.

"There's a natural cave system that runs under the whole headland here," he went on, grinning at them all so widely, Amelia saw gold teeth glinting at the back. "Don't really understand why, but something down there in the caves messes with electronics. You'll have a hard time tuning a radio, much less a TV, and you can forget about using a phone."

"Brilliant," said James. "No wonder it's called Forgotten Bay."

Amelia *almost* felt sorry for her brother. He was taking a college-level class in electronic engineering at school, and whenever he wasn't chatting online to his friends or rewriting the operating system on their computer, he was working on his engineering class project. With no electronics here, James would have nothing.

Then Amelia realized it wasn't James she should feel sorry for – if he couldn't have his gadgets, computers and constant superfast broadband, James wouldn't suffer alone. He'd make sure everyone else suffered along with him.

Tom turned to Dad. "Sorry I wasn't here when you arrived. I had some ... business that kept me."

"No worries!" Dad bounced right back to cheerful again. "We've only been here long enough to stretch our legs." He reached over to Tom and held out his hand in greeting. "Scott Walker."

As Tom gripped Dad's hand and shook it, Amelia saw that something was wrong with the caretaker's fingers. The shake was quick, and Tom put his hand back in his pocket too fast for Amelia to get a second look, but there was *something* ...

"This is my wife, Skye," Dad went on. "And the kids, James and Amelia."

Tom nodded. "Let's get you inside, then. I think Lady Naomi is out already, so don't worry about making noise."

"Lady who?" asked Amelia.

"She must be the standing reservation," Mum said. "How long has she been staying here?"

A strange, distant look passed over Tom's face. "Oh, err, quite a while now," he said, rifling through a tool belt that seemed to have more springs and wires in it than screwdrivers or pliers. He pulled out a huge bunch of keys, and Amelia tried to watch without obviously staring. "But she keeps to herself mostly. Busy with her research project."

"Should've researched herself a better place to stay," said James, as Tom flicked through the keys one by one.

Tom mustn't have heard. "Lady N. will come and go, but she's no trouble at all. Not like some guests, eh?" He cracked a strange grin at Dad. "Ah, here it is!"

Tom held a huge brass key and limped up the steps to the double doors of the main entrance.

He fumbled with the lock, then gave the door a rough shove with the palm of his right hand. Amelia blinked.

The door swung open with a creak.

"After you," said Tom, and ushered the Walkers into their new home.

Amelia stepped past Tom to go into the hotel, flinching a little. Whatever it was about the hotel that creeped her out, Tom had it in bucketfuls.

If possible, the inside of the place was even dustier, dirtier and more disheveled than the outside. Old, darkened oil paintings hung on the walls in heavy gold frames. Two huge stone staircases rose up from the lobby floor, one curving around to the left wing of the hotel, the other to the right, and in the middle, a giant chandelier hung over them like a crystal death trap, just waiting for someone to loosen the pin that held it to its chain. It was amazing that anything so rich and elegant could look so spooky and foul at the same time.

"Thank goodness we've got Mary coming on Monday," said Mum. "This is far more than the quick vacuum and coat of paint you promised, Scott."

Dad scratched the back of his neck and smiled awkwardly.

But Amelia wasn't listening. She was remembering Tom's hand pushing open the front door. She had finally realized what was wrong with it.

One of his fingers was missing.

CHAPTER TWO

"Aaargh!"

Metal crashed to the ground, followed by the sound of shattering glass. There was a moment's silence, and then Dad called out, "I'm OK!"

Amelia and James looked at each other. James rolled his eyes. Amelia yawned hugely. She thought she'd been exhausted yesterday, but that was nothing compared to how she felt after her first night sleeping in the hotel. Or *not* sleeping.

She'd had to drag herself down to breakfast in the staff room, a cozy, almost normal-looking room off the hotel's huge kitchen. It was the only room Amelia had seen so far that wasn't either enormous (the kitchen, the ballroom, the library) or crammed full of shabby antiques and half-ruined heirlooms (the dining room, the lounge, the main bedrooms), or both.

Sitting with James, eating cereal around the ordinary pine table from their old kitchen, Amelia could pretend she was at home. Except for the plates and plates of food crowding out their cereal bowls, that is. Bumping up against each other were dishes of gray, watery scrambled eggs, fried eggs with bits of shell cooked into the whites, French toast that was amazingly burnt and raw at the same time, greasy bacon strips ...

Amelia shuddered and turned back to her cornflakes. She didn't want to hurt Dad's feelings, but it was too early in the day for her to deal with his breakfast menu experiments.

There was another shriek from the kitchen, and the gush of a fire extinguisher discharging. Amelia paused with her spoon in midair. The smoke alarms began to screech.

"Well, at least we know *something* works," said Amelia, covering her ears.

"Whose idea was it for Dad to be the cook?" James sighed, poking warily at a blueberry muffin with liquid batter oozing out of the berry holes.

The alarms cut off and Amelia put her hands down. "Not mine," she said. "I always thought he was supposed to be really good at his old job. I don't know why he thought this would be better."

James nodded. "I asked Mum if Dad had been fired, and that's why we had to come here."

Amelia's eyes widened. She'd been so sure this move from the city had been about James, it hadn't occurred to her there might be another reason. "Dad was fired?"

25

"Mum said no. Actually, she said this is a kind of promotion for Dad."

Amelia stared at him. That made no sense at all.

Dad was a scientist. He worked in a government lab with gigantic computers and telescopes and machines that studied outer space, and dozens of assistants who talked about ideas so insanely complicated that it was like they were speaking another language. So how did moving out to the edge of nowhere and burning eggs for a living make sense as a *promotion*?

Mum burst in through the door. "What's happening? Fire?"

James just pointed towards the door on the other side of the room. "Dad."

Mum sighed. Amelia couldn't tell if it was relief or exasperation.

"Scott?" she called. "Do you need help?"

Dad popped his head around the kitchen door. "I'm fine!" He waved happily. A dish towel was wrapped around his hand, and Amelia saw that it was blotched with blood. "Just learning the ropes."

Mum raised her eyebrows, and followed Dad into the kitchen. "Come on, then. Tell me what you've done to your hand."

Amelia looked at James. "Definitely wasn't a promotion for Mum."

James shook his head in agreement. Mum had had to quit her job as a diplomat to come here. And she *loved* being a diplomat.

There was another strange noise – this time a low, groaning buzz that came from the front of the hotel.

Mum poked her head out, puzzled. "What was that? Oh!" Her face cleared. "The doorbell. It must need a new battery."

After Tom's comment the day before, Amelia had been worried the hotel had no electricity at all. She'd been dreading (silently, of course, no need to tell anyone) a night in a deserted hotel with only candlelight, but it turned out the electricity was running fine. Simple things like the lights and hot water and the toaster worked without a hitch, but just as Tom had warned, anything more complicated – a computer, microwave, even a bedside clock – seemed to act very weirdly.

James had tried all night to text his friends, testing different locations around the hotel, going out in the grounds, even climbing onto the roof, but in the end he'd given up.

Mum walked out to the lobby, and there was an ominous creak as she opened the main doors to the hotel. Amelia stayed where she was. She had enough new things to think about without seeing who was at the door.

Five seconds later, though, a boy about her age exploded through the staff room door, bellowing, "Whoa! This place is awesome!"

James just stared at him, like he was way too cool and grown-up to respond, but Amelia couldn't help grinning.

"Charlie!" called a voice from outside. "Slow down! Where are you?"

Mum came back into the staff room with another woman, just as Dad wandered out of the kitchen. Somehow, his trousers were now wet to the knees and he had flour in his hair.

When he saw the boy and his mum, he smiled cheerfully. "Hello, you caught me making bread."

"Scott," said Mum. "This is Mary Floros, and her son, Charlie." She turned to Amelia and James. "Mary's going to be helping us around the hotel."

"Hey!" Charlie sat himself down next to Amelia, and before she could warn him he took a cinnamon roll. He bit into it, crinkled up his nose in surprise, and then shrugged and kept chewing.

The adults wandered off to Mum's office to talk business.

"Hi," said Amelia, quietly. "I'm Amelia, and this is –"

"James," said Charlie, muffled by the half a roll

in his mouth. "Yeah, I know. Mum told me." He grabbed her arm, swallowed hard and said, "I can't believe he's real!"

"Who?" said Amelia. "James?"

"No!" Charlie snorted. "The caretaker! The old guy with the eye patch! We passed him on the driveway. Oh man, I thought he was just a story!"

"That's Tom," said Amelia.

"I know," said Charlie. "Well, I mean, if that's even his *real* name."

"Did you see his hand?" Amelia asked, making a face. "He's missing a finger – *creepy*."

"*So* creepy," Charlie sighed happily. "I can't believe you get to live here. Have you explored everything yet?" He gave up on the cinnamon roll and dropped it into a bowl of oatmeal.

"No, we've only been here a day. We picked our rooms, unpacked the car, and then the trucks arrived with all our boxes, and –"

"So let's go!" Charlie interrupted, standing up suddenly. "I saw a bunch of hedges out there. I bet they're an old maze! I love mazes! I mean, I've never been in one, but I bet I love them!"

James grunted. "Good idea. Get out of the house for a while."

Amelia spotted the look on her brother's face. She could always tell when he was up to something, and this time she was pretty sure she knew what. James wanted to lurk around the house and see what Lady Naomi looked like.

Hoo boy ...

Back home, James had fallen in love with plenty of girls just by looking at them. As far as Amelia knew, though, this was the first time he'd fallen in love with a girl just from the sound of her name.

"You know," Amelia said quietly to her brother, "Lady Naomi could turn out to be a hundred years old. With warts."

"Lady who?" said Charlie.

James glowered at them both.

Amelia got up from the table. "Hey, how about that maze, Charlie?"

"Yeah!" Charlie was already bounding to the door. "See ya, James."

Amelia laughed as she ran after him. Charlie seemed kind of nuts, but he was definitely going to be fun to have around. Maybe she wouldn't feel quite so worried or spooked by the hotel with him charging around the place.

They ran together through the lobby, and for the first time since they'd arrived, the booming echo of footsteps in the empty space didn't feel lonely. They were just sprinting at full pelt through the doors, about to leap off the top step of the veranda to the driveway below, when Charlie's mum let out a piercing whistle.

Charlie stopped dead. "Oh, man."

Amelia saw all three parents wander out of the hotel.

"Time to go, Charlie," his mum called.

"But we only just got here!"

"And we don't start until tomorrow, so why don't we give Amelia and her family some time to themselves?"

"But –"

"Charlie, I'll be working here every day of the week, and you'll be coming here every day after school with Amelia, but that won't start until *tomorrow*."

Charlie heaved a sigh. "OK. See you in class tomorrow, Amelia."

"How do you know we'll be in the same class?"

"What do you mean?" said Charlie. "Of course we'll be in the same class. You'll see."

CHAPTER THREE

"Dad!" Amelia yelled out the door. "Can you help me?"

"What is it?"

"I want to take this picture down. I don't like it in my room."

Amelia heard Dad's footsteps on the staircase outside. She took a deep breath and looked around her new bedroom, cluttered with all her half-unpacked bags and the boxes with her name on them.

The room was more than twice as big as her

old one, with a big bay window that jutted out over the hotel grounds like the bow of a boat. The window had a seat built into it, and when she sat there she could see over one side of the headland, the bush, and out to the sea beyond. With enough cushions, it would be like sitting in a cloud.

Her old bed was on the other side of the room. In the far corner, Dad had shoved the original bed against the wall – an antique four-poster bed, with carved columns and faded pink-and-green curtains, but no mattress. Dad had promised they would get a new mattress for it and wash the curtains so Amelia could use it.

"When we get settled," Mum had added. Whatever that meant.

Anyway, it was a good room, and it had the potential to be a great room. The only thing Amelia didn't like was the giant old portrait on the wall. It was of a lady in old-fashioned clothes, who somehow managed to look kind and gentle and vaguely sinister all at the same time.

The place had felt much worse last night. The hotel was OK in the daytime, with sun pouring in through the windows and birds singing like everything was right in the world. In the dark, though, in a room filled with unfamiliar shadows, the hotel had been a very freaky place indeed. Last night, Amelia had lain awake in bed for hours, listening to things gnawing in the walls and wild animals fighting in the ceilings. To tell the truth, she'd kept the light on all night.

"Ah," said Dad, appearing in the doorway. "Matilda Swervingthorpe."

"Who?" said Amelia.

"Her," said Dad, pointing at the painting. "She was the original owner of this place, back before it was a hotel."

"Oh," said Amelia. "She looks ancient. She

didn't, uh, die here or anything, did she? Like, in this room ...?"

Not that she believed in ghosts.

"What? Oh, no, she definitely didn't die here."

There was something odd about the way Dad said that.

Amelia asked, "*Definitely* not here? Why? Where did she die?"

"Well ... that's kind of a funny story, actually," Dad said. He kept his back to her and heaved the painting off the wall, leaving behind a rectangle of wallpaper that was still fresh and colorful compared to the rest of the walls. A couple of dried-out eucalyptus leaves fell away and fluttered to the ground. "It turns out no one's quite sure *what* happened to Matilda. She seems to have gone missing."

"Missing?" said Amelia, who didn't see how that was funny at all. "What do you mean –"

But then another mystery pulled her attention. As Dad set the picture down on the floor, Amelia saw that he had also uncovered a small metal door, set into the wall. It had been hidden behind the painting just like a safe in a cartoon.

"Ooh, look!" said Dad. "We might have treasure in here." He tried the handle. "Locked, of course. I wonder if we can find the combination. I'll ask Tom."

"No!" Amelia blurted.

Dad looked at her curiously. "You don't want me to ask Tom?"

Amelia winced. Dad seemed to think Tom was a "character." She didn't want to be rude, but she didn't trust Tom. You couldn't exactly blame someone for having an eye patch, or missing a finger, or walking with a limp, or for being really old, or having gold teeth, and Amelia knew you should never judge people for how they looked, but …

Well, sorry, but Tom was just creepy.

"Um," she stalled. "I just need to get my room sorted out first. I guess the door can wait ..."

Wait until Dad forgot about asking Tom, that is.

"All right," said Dad. "Suit yourself." He hefted the portrait in both hands. Grunting under the weight of the painting, Dad shuffled sideways out of the room.

Amelia shivered and went back to her bed. Outside, it was a perfect day. Too good to be stuck in here really, no matter how much unpacking Mum wanted her to get through.

Amelia was feeling a bit flat since Charlie had left. She wasn't the sort of kid who made friends that easily – back home, she'd always needed a while to warm up and get comfortable with people before she could relax and just hang out. But here, where everything around her was a combination of old, dirty, broken and spooky, Charlie had been the only part that looked cheerful and uncomplicated.

She lay back on her bed and gazed at the cobwebs on the ceiling, wishing she could go to sleep and let the rest of the day pass by without her. It was so quiet here – no traffic, no sounds of construction sites or kids yelling at the skate park – nothing but the dull wash of the surf on the cliffs below, and the buzzing of a fly against the window.

And a creak of wooden floorboards.

She sat up in bed, her heart hammering. She peered out of her window in time to see a dark shape emerge from under the far end of the veranda. It was Tom. She watched him limp down the stairs, then cross the lawn, heading down the hill towards those dark, towering trees.

Amelia had seen him come and go a few times already today. She was surprised he hadn't worn a path as he hurried back and forth. He never seemed to stay long at the hotel. Once he was carrying a box draped in an old sack; once he talked in quiet tones to Mum; and a couple of other times Amelia only saw him as he was leaving. But no matter how many times Amelia saw him, the uneasy hitch in her stomach never wore off.

Tom had said his cottage was hidden back there among the trees somewhere, so it made sense he was going in that direction. It even made sense that he would have been hanging around the hotel. That was his job after all, right?

But something in the way Tom kept appearing and disappearing, always in a hurry, made Amelia nervous. She slid off her bed and tiptoed to the bay window. She held her breath, although there was no way Tom could hear her from all the way down there. No way at all.

Which was why she let out a little scream of

surprise when he suddenly looked back over his shoulder and stared up at the window, straight into her eyes.

Amelia dropped to the floor, and lay crouched beside the window seat, panting in shock and fear. How had he known she was there? And worse: had she just made an enemy of him?

She was still lying there, shaking, when Dad walked back in.

"Amelia, I – where are you? Oh, hello, you funny thing. What are you doing down there?"

"I – um … I –"Amelia sat up and tried to slow her breathing. "Dad." She came to a decision. "Dad, I just saw Tom out my window. He'd been at the hotel, and he was rushing away, and he looked at me."

Dad took a step back. "He looked at you? What do you mean? When?"

"Just then. Out the window."

"You mean, you were up here, and he was down there, and then he looked at you?"

"Yes."

"While you were looking at him?"

"Yes."

"OK," Dad laughed. "Well, as Gran used to say, a cat can look at a king. Now about your other crisis – those wild animals you heard in the roof last night. Look!"

He held up a box of rat poison and a massive trap. "Ta-daa!"

"Eww! Dad! In my room?"

Somehow, when Dad sorted things out for Amelia, she usually felt worse.

Amelia's stomach was starting to growl for dinner when the doorbell chimed brightly. Maybe Tom had actually done a real job and fetched batteries for them.

Amelia pushed aside the box she was sorting through and went out to the rail that ran around the upper gallery, overlooking the lobby and front doors. Mum was smoothing down her shirt as she walked to answer the door.

"Is it pizza?" Amelia called.

Mum jumped slightly, then grinned up at Amelia. "No, our first guest!"

"But –"

Mum put a finger to her lips. "Shh!"

Amelia had been about to say, *But we're not open yet*. Fair enough if Mum didn't want the guest to hear that, although it wouldn't take them very long to figure it out. There were still cobwebs dangling from all the lights, and dust bunnies the size of actual bunnies under all the furniture.

Mum opened the door with a flourish. "Welcome to the Gateway Hotel!"

A tall woman dressed in shimmering purple-and-green robes stepped into the lobby, peering anxiously from side to side as though near-sighted. Hopefully she wouldn't notice the mess, then. Her head was covered with an intricately patterned scarf, and Amelia saw chunky beads of different colors flashing at her neck and wrist.

Wow. Who was this woman? She reminded Amelia of a movie star or a princess – and not a boring actual princess, but a fairy-tale princess – someone who belonged in a castle with a moat. Amelia leaned out farther over the railing, and the woodwork let out a creak.

Downstairs, the woman flinched and looked up towards Amelia with an expression that seemed terrified. She squinted, and then, when she realized Amelia was just a kid, the woman took a breath and smiled. An incredibly fake smile. She was clearly freaking out.

Mum smiled very warmly, and said, "You must be Elizabeth Ardman. I'm Skye, the manager here. Can I help you with your luggage?"

Miss Ardman pulled back in alarm, and clutched to her chest the only piece of luggage she had – an old-fashioned leather case, about the size of a bowling bag. "No!"

Mum just kept smiling, totally relaxed. "Of course. Well, let me show you your room. We're in quite a mess as you can see, but I can assure you, Miss Ardman ..."

Mum kept quietly talking on, saying nothing much, but in such a friendly, soothing tone that Miss Ardman began to calm down.

"Please, call me Liz," Amelia heard the guest say, and she was reminded again what an awesome diplomat Mum must have been.

Mum led Miss Ardman up the right-hand stairs, past Lady Naomi's room and so far down the corridor that Amelia could no longer see them. She was just turning to go back to her own room when she saw that the main door downstairs was ajar. Had Mum left it like that? Amelia tried to remember whether it had been closed after Miss Ardman came in.

She was about to go downstairs to close it herself when something moved in the darkness outside the door. What she had assumed to be the black of the night sky was actually a shadow – no, a shape. Somebody was out there, their whole body pressed into the gap in the door.

The door eased open a little wider and a face pushed through, looking up the stairs as if trying to see where Mum and Miss Ardman had gone.

Amelia saw his jaw clench, his brow furrow, as he stared after Miss Ardman with strange intensity.

It was Tom.

CHAPTER FOUR

As soon as Amelia arrived at school the next morning, she saw what Charlie had meant about being in the same class. At her old school, there had been nine kindergarten classes, five grade sixes, and all the grades in between were just as big. She'd assumed school would be the same here. Maybe not quite as many kids as that, but enough that she'd wanted Mum to come with her on the first day.

As they'd walked together, Amelia had tried to say something to Mum about Tom sneaking around after Miss Ardman last night, but Mum told her not to be silly. It was like her parents just couldn't (or wouldn't) see how strange and suspicious he was.

Maybe they're right, Amelia thought. *Maybe I am just imagining it all.*

James had left super early to catch the only bus into the city an hour away. He was going to the high school there, because Forgotten Bay was too small to have its own. That should have tipped Amelia off, but she was still surprised when she and Mum came around the last bend and saw a metal fence around an ordinary-looking house.

Not *that* ordinary. It was painted pink and blue, and the playground was a sloping lawn that ran all the way down to a sandy beach, but it certainly wasn't a normal school building.

Amelia walked through the open gate, scanning her new surroundings and following the path towards the school office – always checking that her mum was close, but not *too* close.

They'd only made it halfway along the path before Charlie bounded up, exactly as joyful and noisy as he'd been the day before.

"Amelia! You're here!" He ran up and grabbed her arm. "Hi, Mrs. Walker," he added, dragging Amelia away with him. "Come on, I told everyone you'd be here today."

She ran with him, but faltered slightly as they turned the corner of the building and she saw the yard behind the school, full of children. Charlie yelled out, and everyone turned to look.

In a split second, Amelia knew two things: that thanks to Charlie, she was now the center of attention for about forty kids who were complete strangers; and – judging by the looks on some of their faces – Charlie might not be the best person to be doing the introducing.

"So," Charlie beamed, apparently oblivious to the fact that Amelia had stopped dead behind him. "Everyone, this is Amelia – her family got here on Saturday. Amelia, this is everyone – so, um, that's Dean, and Callan, and –"

"Hi, I'm Sophie T.," said a girl about Charlie's height, standing at Amelia's side and totally ignoring Charlie. "This is Sophie F., and Shani," she added, indicating two girls behind her.

The three girls smiled at her, waiting, and Amelia blinked and realized she hadn't yet said a word. "Uh, oh – hi! I'm Amelia ... like Charlie said."

Sophie T. ignored the mention of Charlie. She didn't so much as glance at him as she asked, "Did you just move into the hotel?"

Other kids had started to cluster around, listening as Amelia said, "Yes."

"Not the one on the hill?" a boy gasped.

"How many other hotels do we have, dummy?" his friend scoffed.

"But no one lives there – it's haunted!" said someone else.

Amelia stood, dazed. Dozens of questions were flying at her now – about Tom (Charlie was right, Tom seemed to be a local legend – a sort of cross between Bigfoot and the bogeyman), about ghosts, about why they'd come, where she'd come from, how long she'd be staying, and most of all, over and over again, "Aren't you afraid to sleep there?"

At some point a bell rang and Amelia supposed Mum must have left. She was nowhere to be seen when they started lining up for assembly, anyway.

Assembly was on the lawn under a huge sail tied up as a shade cloth. Forgotten Bay Primary had two classes: upper and lower. Mr. Whitlock took the lower class, and Amelia was with Ms. Slaviero in the upper.

"Good morning, everyone!" said Ms. Slaviero. "I'm sure you've all noticed by now, we have a new student starting today. Amelia Walker, won't you come up to the front and introduce yourself?"

Amelia would rather have made a run for it into the bushes, but she walked from her place, past all the kids, and up to Ms. Slaviero.

"Settle down, thank you," said Ms. Slaviero, waiting for quiet. "Now, Amelia, tell us about yourself."

"Um … well," said Amelia, thinking this was somewhat ridiculous. She'd done nothing but tell people about herself since she'd arrived, but anyway … "I'm Amelia, and my family just moved into the Gateway Hotel."

To her surprise, the kids were all listening, rapt.

"That's nice," Ms. Slaviero said, encouragingly. "Did you live in another hotel before coming here?"

"Um, no," said Amelia. "My mum is a diplomat, and my dad is a scientist. Or was. I don't know."

"A scientist!" Ms. Slaviero was suddenly more excited than the kids. "What sort?"

"Some kind of astrophysicist," said Amelia.

Ms. Slaviero let out a little yelp of delight. "An astrophysicist? My favorite! We'll have to invite him to give a talk! We could show him our telescopes! Oh, this is too good!"

Amelia was eventually allowed to rejoin her class. For the rest of assembly, kids kept turning around to stare at her. Some of them looked at her with curiosity, others with pity, and some with a strange sort of dread. It was becoming pretty clear that living in the Gateway Hotel was a massive deal in Forgotten Bay.

As they walked to class, Charlie was begging, "Can Amelia sit with me, Ms. Slaviero? Can she? Please?"

Amelia hadn't thought about this, but now that Charlie had brought it up, she was worried. She liked Charlie, she really did. She could already tell that he was funny and kind and generous. But she could also tell that being stuck with Charlie at school would make it harder for her to make friends with other people. Even saying that to herself felt disloyal and mean, but she knew it was also true.

Luckily for Amelia, Ms. Slaviero said, "Sorry, Charlie, we've already got ten kids on the Dark Side of the room, and only nine on the Light Side. I need to put Amelia with the Sophies and Shani to bring balance to the Force."

Amelia saw disappointment on Charlie's face, but she couldn't help a little guilty sigh of relief.

As she unpacked her pencil case and put her books into her desk, the three girls whispered at her over the top of one another. "How old are you?" "Do you have any brothers or sisters?" "Do you have a boyfriend?" "What grade were you in at your old school?" "How many –"

Smiling to herself, Amelia chanced a quick look across the room at Charlie. He caught her eye and sadly shook his head, as if profoundly sorry for her.

By recess, Amelia had learned that Sophie T.'s sister's rabbit was having babies, that Shani had a twin brother (Dean), and that yo-yos and skipping rope were out, but trading cards and handball were in. And she had told them in return about doing gymnastics, and that she had a seventeen-year-old brother. With no encouragement from Amelia, all the girls had decided that he was probably gorgeous.

Out of the corner of her eye, Amelia saw Charlie with a group of boys. She heard them joking around, talking about someone.

"My dad reckons he's a criminal," said one boy. "Why else would he spend his whole life hiding out at that dump?"

"Maybe because he's so ugly he's embarrassed for anyone to see him?" suggested Dean.

With a thrill of horror, Amelia realized they were discussing Tom.

"No," said another. "It's because he's gone crazy. My brother went up there once at night on a dare, and he heard Tom shouting to himself – like a real argument – but no one else was there."

"I know what he is," said Charlie. "Isn't it obvious? Eye patch, missing finger, he walks with a limp – he's a pirate!"

The boys recoiled as Charlie spoke, and Dean snorted, "A pirate? Are you six years old?"

The other boys laughed. Not really cruelly, not really to be mean, but just because, Amelia could tell, they thought Charlie was an idiot. She winced in sympathy, but was soon drawn back to the Sophies' conversation.

The rest of the day was a blur until after the final bell, when Amelia was free to walk with Charlie back to the hotel.

"Sucks that you got stuck with the Sophies," said Charlie as they walked along the beach road.

"They're all right."

"Sophie F.'s all right, maybe. When she's on her own. But Sophie T. is *so* bad."

"Well, she was nice to me."

Charlie made a disgusted sound. "Whatever."

"Anyway," said Amelia, puffing slightly as they began to climb the steep road up to the headland. "Guess what happened last night? A guest arrived."

"But we're not open yet."

"I know."

"So how come –"

"I don't know," Amelia interrupted. "But that's not the weird part."

She told Charlie about Tom running back and forth to the hotel before the guest arrived, and then how jumpy and strange the woman had been, and then how Tom had been spying on her through the door.

"Spying on the guest, or on your mum?" asked Charlie.

"I don't know, but he was definitely spying and not just looking."

Charlie thought about that. "If Tom is a pirate, he's probably planning to rob her."

Amelia almost rolled her eyes. They turned off the road, and up the long gravel driveway to the hotel. Past the overgrown rose gardens, Amelia nudged Charlie. "That's her."

Miss Ardman was lying on an old lounge chair by the fountain, her face turned up to the hot afternoon sun.

"Hope she's wearing sunblock," said Amelia. "You really would expect an adult to be more sensible about their skin, wouldn't you?"

But Charlie wasn't listening, let alone looking at Miss Ardman. He'd been distracted by something glinting in the grass on the other side of the driveway and had gone to investigate.

"Hey, check this out," he said.

It was a black cylinder, with brass rings at each end and more rings in the middle.

"What is that?" asked Amelia.

"I don't know."

"It looks like lipstick for a robot."

Charlie looked at her scornfully,

which irritated Amelia. She'd been far more polite about his silly pirate comments. He played with the thing for a minute, then shrugged and slipped it into his pocket. He took two more steps up the hill, glanced over at Miss Ardman (at last), and froze.

He gazed for a long while at Miss Ardman. Then he looked up at the hotel. Then down the driveway they'd just walked up. Then back at the hotel.

"So, where's her car?"

"What?"

"If she arrived last night, how did she get here? Where's her car?"

Amelia shrugged. "Taxi?"

"In Forgotten Bay?" Charlie laughed. "What taxi?"

"I don't know, I didn't hear any car."

"Well, then how did she get here? Parachute?

Bicycle? She can't have *walked* ..."

Amelia realized it wasn't just the car. The whole scene seemed weird – wrong. Who would come to a hotel before it was open, or even clean, just to do some sunbathing? The beach must have been just a short walk away, why not go there?

They trudged up the steps to the main entrance. Amelia was sweaty and weary, and didn't care about how Miss Ardman had traveled. All she could think about was getting a popsicle, pronto.

But once they had their popsicles, something very strange happened.

Amelia and Charlie had both kicked off their shoes and socks in the staff room on their way to the freezer, so their bare feet were soundless on the marble staircase. They were so busy sucking on their popsicles, that Charlie (amazingly) wasn't talking. And Amelia, who was secretly very curious about Lady Naomi and looking for any excuse to go past her room, had taken Charlie up the staircase on the guests' side of the hotel. So they were in exactly the right place at the right time to see Tom come out of a guest's bedroom.

Amelia gripped Charlie's arm and silently pointed at Tom. They watched him ease the door shut behind him and limp along the corridor to the back of the hotel.

Amelia's scalp prickled. She knew which room Tom had just snuck out of.

Miss Ardman's.

CHAPTER FIVE

Charlie opened his mouth to shout, but Amelia clamped her palm over his face.

"Mmph, get off!" Charlie hissed, pulling Amelia's hand away. "He's stealing or something!"

"Maybe, but you can't just –"

She broke off, watching as Tom limped around a corner and out of sight. Amelia's chest tightened. Tom was meant to be working for her parents. He was meant to be mowing the lawns, trimming the hedges and keeping the tennis courts swept. He was *not* meant to be letting himself into the hotel and prowling around the guest quarters. She tried to be logical, and not give way to the anger swirling inside.

"He *could* just be doing some repair work," she whispered. "Maybe there was a pipe in that room that needed fixing or something."

"Then where were his tools?" said Charlie. "And why be all sneaky about it? Come on, let's see where he's going!"

"Yeah, OK," said Amelia. "But *quietly*. We don't want him to –"

Charlie, though, had already bolted along the corridor. Amelia followed, heart pounding. They ran past a dozen or more closed doors before the corridor turned and they were in the servants' end of the wing. Here were the linen cupboards, a storeroom for brooms and mops, and the start of narrow stairs that led down the back of the hotel. And Tom.

His hand was gripping the banister, one foot out in space and ready to descend. He started at the sight of them. None of those gold tooth-flashing smiles now. Just a glowering one-eyed scowl.

Charlie and Amelia stopped abruptly, then Charlie said, "What are you doing, sneaking around up here?"

Amelia thought that was brave, but also extremely rude, seeing as Charlie had never actually met Tom before.

Tom's eyes widened for a moment, but then his face crumpled back into an angry grimace. "I could ask you the same question."

"Us?" said Amelia, trying to keep her voice steady. "I *live* here! What about you?"

Tom raised an eyebrow. "I live here too, and I have done for far longer than you have, Amelia."

Amelia swallowed, suddenly wishing they'd never come up here.

"So what?" said Charlie. "You think that gives you the right to –"

"To do my job? To attend to hotel business?" said Tom calmly. "Yeah, I think it does."

Charlie glanced sideways at Amelia. She felt the look but refused to return it. She was too busy trying to will herself invisible.

"Now," Tom continued, "why don't you kids move along? I don't think your parents would be too happy to find you snooping around the guest quarters, do you?"

And with that, he limped heavily down the stairs. Amelia closed her eyes, stomach twisting. If she'd been on the wrong side of Tom before, what did he think of her *now*?

"Amelia?" Mum called from the other end of the hotel. "Is that you home? Have you got Charlie with you?"

They ran back to the gallery end of the corridor

and leaned over the railing to see her looking out from the library, a phone pressed to her ear. The phone cord stretched tight behind her, so she couldn't come out any farther.

"Mum!" Amelia was flooded with relief. "Tom was up here – in Miss Ardman's room!"

"Tom? Really?" Mum frowned.

Amelia and Charlie glanced at each other.

"I hope you two didn't bother him while he was working," said Mum, taking away any thread of hope she'd be on their side. "Oh, err, hang on." She turned her attention to the phone. "I'm sorry, could you just give me a moment? Well, yes, I know I was waiting on hold for you, but now I just need thirty seconds to – right, very kind of you, I'm sure." She covered the mouthpiece, and turned back to them. "Look, never mind, I've got to take this. But don't distract Tom, OK? You can see how much work this place needs before we can open."

"But, Mum –"

Mum held up a finger. "Not now. Go on – scoot. I'm busy."

"Come on, Charlie," muttered Amelia. "Let's go to my room."

"*Hotel business,*" Charlie sneered, following her across the gallery to the family wing. "Yeah, right! As if *that's* what Tom was doing!"

"Yeah," Amelia breathed. She crept into her room and over to the bay window, beckoning Charlie to follow. "That's why I want to see where he goes."

"Why are you whispering?" said Charlie, in his usual voice.

"Shh!"

Amelia crouched on the window seat, and saw Tom trudge down the steps, then pause and glare at the hotel. He took a step back towards them, then thought better of it and continued across the grass in the direction of his house.

"Go on," Amelia murmured. "Keep going ... don't hang around here ..."

Finally, Tom stomped off down the driveway and across the lawn to the magnolia trees.

Amelia breathed a sigh of relief.

"You know," said Charlie, "Tom must have seen that woman sunbathing. We did."

"Miss Ardman? So?"

"So, if Tom knew she was out *there*, then what did he want in *here*? If it were really *hotel business* then he would have just told her, right, and come up and down the front stairs like a normal person. But he was sneaking. And the only reason I can think of to sneak is because he's a thief. He wants to go through her bags."

"She only brought one. And it was like a big handbag, it wasn't a proper suitcase or anything."

"Well, I bet you anything," Charlie said, "that whatever is in that bag is worth a fortune and Tom is trying to steal it."

It wasn't completely clear to Amelia how Charlie had talked her into it, but two minutes later, there she was – creeping around behind the front desk of the hotel, searching for the spare key to Miss Ardman's room. She scanned the wall behind the desk. It was covered in dozens of wooden pigeonholes, each with a brass room number above the opening. Back in the hotel's heyday these tiny niches were used to hold guests' mail or phone messages. Right now, they just housed the keys.

Getting the key was easy. Mum had locked the partition that closed off access to the reception desk, but after six years of gymnastics, that was hardly a barrier to Amelia. She sprang lightly over it, grabbed the cold length of the key, and jumped back over without a sound. She ran back to Charlie and threw the key in his lap.

"Gee, it's a heavy old thing, isn't it?" said Charlie, examining it. "You were great, Amelia! You could be a professional cat burglar."

Amelia was horrified. "Don't say that!" She paused. "Charlie, I don't know if I can go through with this. If we go sneaking around in Miss Ardman's room, how are we any better than Tom?"

"So, what then?"

Amelia bit her lip. "Maybe we should put it back."

"OK," Charlie said simply.

"What?"

"OK, let's put the key back."

"Really?"

"Sure. No problem. We put back the key, and

we forget about getting evidence, and you can just *trust* that Tom is honest and trustworthy and safe to have around your family and your stuff. You can just *trust* that he's a good guy, while you sleep alone in this big hotel, far from town ..."

Amelia snatched the key out of Charlie's hands. "Fine. Give me that." She stalked up the stairs.

Charlie scurried after her. "We're only going to look, anyway," he whispered. "We're not going to touch anything, and no one will ever know, so there's no harm, and –"

"Hush, Charlie," Amelia hissed.

They trod quietly past Lady Naomi's room, though Amelia had no idea whether she was in there or not. Maybe Lady Naomi didn't even exist. She could just be a story Tom had invented to cover up some pirate secret. Amelia considered it a very bad sign that Charlie's silly pirate theory was starting to feel at home in her brain.

Charlie nudged her. "We could get the key to that room next."

Amelia didn't even bother to say "hush" this time.

They walked past several more doors until they came to the room Miss Ardman was using. Amelia knocked quietly. There was no response.

"Housekeeping!" squealed Charlie in a piercing falsetto voice, pounding on the door with his fist.

"Be quiet!" whispered Amelia, her voice shrill with fear. But when no one answered, she had to admit, she was glad Charlie had checked too.

"She must be still outside," said Charlie. "It's safe to go in."

Amelia gripped the key. She told herself they *had* to do this, that Mum and Dad were so convinced Tom was trustworthy, the only way they were going to convince them otherwise was if they had some hard evidence he was up to ...

well, whatever he was up to.

She took a deep breath, and unlocked the door.

Inside, the room was empty. It was better than a lot of the other rooms on this wing, but still shabby, dusty and musty.

Amelia wondered again why anyone would come to stay in this dump.

"Look at that," Charlie whispered, stepping past Amelia and into the room.

On the dressing table, where hairbrushes and vases of flowers would usually be, was a small glass tank. Like a fish tank, but not for fish. This tank was filled with enormous, glistening centipedes. The room was so quiet, Amelia could hear the sound of their hundreds of legs as they crawled over one another.

She turned away, trying not to gag. "Just find the bag. Is it still here?"

Charlie didn't answer. He was pacing towards

the enormous canopy bed at the far end of the room, a funny look on his face.

"Do you feel that?" he murmured.

"Feel what?" said Amelia, moving to join him. Then she paused, a strange sensation washing over her as she approached the bed, like a gust of warm spring air. She glanced over at the window, but it was shut tight.

"It's coming from here," said Charlie, crouching at the foot of the bed. He dragged out Miss Ardman's little case. "Wow – it's warm. Touch it!"

Amelia knelt beside him and put a hand on the case. It was definitely warm. Whatever was inside it was hot – or being heated. They hauled the case onto the bed and Amelia felt her head spinning slightly, that strange warmth drifting over her again. Quickly, she unzipped the case and threw back the top of it. A cloud of sweet, perfumed air rose to the ceiling as they stared at what was inside.

"Jewels!" said Charlie breathlessly.

There were twenty or perhaps thirty shining globes, about the size of tangerines, but perfectly round and golden. At first Amelia thought they were reflecting the light that fell on them, but as she leaned closer she realized that the jewels themselves were shimmering – light was glowing from them.

She was too mesmerized to check Charlie's face, but she heard him sigh. "Wow."

Amelia leaned even closer, so close the jewels warmed her cheeks.

She smiled with happiness just to see them. As she breathed in their delicious fragrance, she was filled with a wonderful knowledge: that if she could touch one of those jewels, just hold it in her hand for one moment, she would never feel sad, or lonely, or worried, or angry again.

As she gently reached out her hand, the jewels seemed to reach back to her. They *wanted* to be with her. They wanted her to have them!

Amelia heard Charlie laugh with joy beside her. And then, as her fingers tingled with anticipation, she suddenly felt a massive, vise-like hand seize her by the shoulder and jerk her back from the jewels. It was so fast and rough that Amelia lost her balance and fell to the ground in shock, blinking. Charlie stumbled and fell beside her.

A voice, raw with anger and danger, roared over them, *"How dare you?"*

CHAPTER SIX

Once, Amelia had done a handstand in her grandparents' living room and lost her balance. As her feet came down, so did a very beautiful glass vase her granny had been given for her sixteenth birthday. When Granny saw the smashed pieces all over the floor, her face had gone white with shock and Amelia had felt so bad she wanted to die.

But that moment – with all the terrible sadness, guilt and shame that Amelia had felt – was *nothing* compared to how bad this moment was. In fact, "moment" didn't cover it. This nightmare seemed to go on forever.

First there was the utter shock of being caught by Miss Ardman. Then that had turned to a steady, throbbing terror as Miss Ardman started shrieking and wailing so hysterically that Amelia was sure she'd gone mad.

But then, when Mum and Mary burst in to see what was happening, Miss Ardman had collapsed into a sobbing mess on the floor, and Mary had taken over the shouting instead. Mostly at Charlie, but Amelia knew she was included. Mary dragged Amelia and Charlie out by the collars of their shirts, berating them all the way to Amelia's room.

Amelia felt so remorseful, so humiliated and so, so *angry* – angry at Charlie for talking her into it, and even angrier at herself for letting him.

Mary left them there, and went back to help

Mum calm down Miss Ardman. It had taken ages before the awful crying stopped. At last, Amelia's door opened again and three severe and disappointed parents came into the room.

"Amelia," said Dad. "Mum and I are so shocked. What were you thinking?"

Amelia just shook her head. All the reasons that had made sense when she and Charlie were talking seemed like nonsense now.

"What you did," Mum said, "going into a guest's room – our first guest! – well, I only hope you understand how wrong it was. And *why* it was wrong."

"I do," Amelia whispered miserably.

"I don't," Charlie said.

Amelia stared at him.

"I don't," he repeated. "I mean, I know it wasn't *right*, but was it really that big a deal?"

Mary gaped at him. "You stole a key from the

front desk, broke into a guest's room and went through her personal belongings. That's a big deal!"

"We only borrowed the key," said Charlie. "And we were just looking."

"For what?" Mary asked. "And what gave you the idea you had any right to look in someone else's room, Charlie? That's trespass!"

Charlie's eyes widened. He obviously hadn't thought of that. Amelia felt her own shame deepen another notch – she'd committed a real crime. Not even James had done something that bad.

"Well," Dad twitched slightly, "I'm not sure we need to get the police involved *just* yet. But you do get it, don't you, Charlie?" Dad squatted down so he was eye level with him. "We have to work together as a team if this hotel is going to run smoothly."

Charlie fidgeted under Dad's gaze.

"Charlie?" Mary snapped when he didn't answer straightaway. "Do you get it? Do you know what Mr. Walker is saying?"

Charlie looked at Amelia's dad. "I think so."

"You'd better know so," said Mary. "He's saying that if you can't behave yourself, we will be off the team, Charlie. I will lose my job. Do you understand *that*?"

Dad pulled back a little. "Well, uh, I wasn't exactly ... I'm not threatening ..."

But Mary was staring hard at her son. If Dad wasn't threatening, Mary surely was. "I'm not joking, Charlie," she said quietly. "I need this job."

Charlie dropped his head and nodded.

Dad clapped him on the shoulder, and stood up. "It's all good, Mary. I'm sure both kids have got it straight now. We'll be smooth sailing from now on."

Amelia glanced at Charlie's hunched shape, and some of her anger at him shifted. Before she knew what she was doing, she heard herself say, "Well, what about Tom?"

"What about him?" said Mum.

"Is he part of the team, too? Does *he* have to change his behavior – because there's something up with him!"

Dad and Mum swapped awkward glances, and Amelia could swear they had both tensed up.

"What are you talking about, Amelia?" Mum asked.

"Tom's up to something. We saw him breaking into Miss Ardman's room!"

"Which you so strongly disapprove of," said Dad, "that you decided to break in yourselves."

Amelia blushed, but kept her chin up.

"We were looking for proof of what Tom was up to. We think he's a thief! We were trying to prove it to you to protect the hotel."

"But you can't stop a bad thing by doing that thing yourself," groaned Mum. "I thought you understood that. Dad and I trust Tom, and yes – he's part of our team. You might not like him, and who knows? Maybe he doesn't like you, but we have to work together." She took a deep breath, and said, "Right, we've made our point, I think. Now, when Miss Ardman's had a chance to recover, I'm going to take you to her, and you can apologize for what you've done." She let out a sigh, and some of the hardness slipped from her expression. "With any luck, we can smooth this whole thing over."

The three parents left the room, closing the bedroom door behind them. Amelia and Charlie stared glumly at each other, neither of them speaking.

Then suddenly, Charlie stood up straighter.

"What?" said Amelia.

"Shh!" hissed Charlie, jumping up from the bed. "Listen!"

He crept across the room and pressed his ear to the door. Amelia followed, and heard Mum speaking in a hushed voice.

"I told you it wouldn't work," she said.

"It will," said Dad. "There's nothing to panic about."

Amelia's eyes narrowed.

"The kids messed up," Dad went on. "In a kid way for kid reasons. Nothing's changed."

"I agree," said Mary. "They're worried about Tom; he's the only issue here. It's Tom we need to sort out for them."

Their voices were fading away now. Amelia heard footsteps creaking down the stairs, and strained to hear as Dad said, "I'll talk to him. Ask him to be more careful. I really don't want the kids finding out any ..."

But his voice faded away, and Amelia couldn't make out the rest. She turned to Charlie, a chill snaking up her back. "Did you hear that?"

Charlie nodded mutely, and Amelia felt the cold sink deeper into her bones. Mum and Dad *knew* what Tom was doing – and they were keeping it from her.

Whatever was going on, they were all in on it together.

CHAPTER SEVEN

"I still think Miss Ardman was overreacting," Charlie said, as they walked home from school the next day. "Get cross about kids in your room – fine. Yell a bit – whatever. But *crying* for half an hour?"

"Charlie ..." Amelia said warningly.

"I'm just saying. It's weird."

Amelia knew it was weird – weird, and also awful, because she couldn't forget that the crying had been their fault. But she didn't want to talk about Miss Ardman. Who cared about Miss

Ardman when she'd just found out she couldn't trust her own parents?

You're being silly, she told herself. *Mum and Dad are good people. If they're keeping a secret from us, that doesn't mean they're bad …*

Unless Tom was blackmailing them into doing something.

But it sounded more like they were in on it with Tom. And Mary too.

What could they all be –?

"And I still can't believe they made us go through with that whole apology thing!" Charlie broke in on her thoughts, oblivious. "How awkward was that! And anyway, we were only trying to *help* Miss Ardman!"

"Oh Charlie, just shut it, will you?" Amelia snapped, surprising even herself.

"Fine," said Charlie holding up his hands in mock surrender. "*Sorry.*"

Amelia hadn't spoken to Charlie at all at school. She didn't *avoid* him exactly; it was just easier to let the Sophies and Shani carry her along with their chatter, and pretend she couldn't see Charlie trying to catch her eye. Once he came right over to where they were sitting, but when Amelia ignored him and Sophie T. said in her coldest voice, "Excuse me, Charlie, can we help you?" he went away and didn't try again.

Amelia didn't feel good about it.

On the other hand, school was the one place she could just sit and think through what was going on at the hotel without worrying that something *else* was about to start happening. And even though she knew Charlie wanted to discuss the same thing, even though he was the only person in the world who could possibly understand what was going on in her head, Amelia wanted some space to figure it out by herself. After all, if she couldn't rely on her parents anymore, she might as well get used to being on her own.

By the time the bell rang for home time, Amelia had gone over the facts about five hundred times, but they still didn't make any more sense to her. She had a whole lot of homework that didn't make sense to her either (she might not have been listening very much in class), and Sophie T. was a bit distant with her when they said good-bye to each other at the gate. Amelia got the impression she might have zoned out a few too many times.

So when she saw Charlie waiting for her by the big tree outside school, she was ready to talk to him again. She even smiled when the first words out of his mouth were, "We really need to figure out the deal with Tom."

They dawdled along the footpath past the beach, paused for a moment at the Forgotten Bay

Newsstand (which also sold housewares and collected dry cleaning) while Charlie bought some licorice ropes, and then headed up the steep hill to the Gateway Hotel headland. Neither of them could come up with a better theory to explain Tom sneaking around than Charlie's original pirate idea.

As they got to the hotel steps, Amelia saw that James was already home. He was sitting leaning against a pillar, a dazed expression on his face.

"You're home early," said Amelia.

"Hmmm?" said James. "What? Oh, I had a free period, so I caught the early bus."

Amelia studied him. "Are you OK, James? You seem a little ..."

"Huh? Oh, I'm fine." He smiled to himself. "I'm super."

He stared dreamily into space, his long arms propped on the points of his knees, and a strange pink blush passed over his face.

Amelia suddenly recognized the look. "James, who's here?"

The pink blush on James's face deepened to red. "She just walked right past me. Right there." He stroked the step beside him. "She said hello."

"Who?" said Charlie, baffled.

James sighed. "Lady Naomi."

Amelia rolled her eyes. "Let me guess: *not* a hundred years old?"

"No ..." James closed his eyes and smiled to himself.

"Ugh, come on, Charlie." Amelia walked into the hotel. James was ridiculous. All the same, she couldn't help looking up towards Lady Naomi's room. She was pretty curious herself.

But Lady Naomi must have already disappeared into her room, because the only person around was Miss Ardman. Amelia flinched with embarrassment, but when she saw Miss Ardman holding her bag at the top of the stairs, Amelia found herself smiling. Simply remembering the jewels inside gave her a warm feeling.

Without noticing it, she stepped towards the stairs, closer to Miss Ardman.

Miss Ardman smiled nervously and backed away from the gallery railing. "Hello, children."

"Hello," said Amelia.

"Yeah, hi," said Charlie. His voice sounded as happy and dreamy as James's. As happy and dreamy as Amelia felt.

They both stepped closer again to the stairs, still smiling up at Miss Ardman. But Miss Ardman, her eyes widening in alarm, pulled away from the gallery railing and hurried off to her room. Amelia suddenly felt cold.

"Overreactor," Charlie muttered.

Amelia elbowed him grumpily, and they headed

for the kitchen.

"Hey, kids," said Dad, his apron and eyebrows white with flour. "Cookie?"

He held up a baking tray of surprisingly tasty-smelling cookies, fresh from the oven.

"Ooh, yeah!" said Charlie. His mood shifted quickly in the presence of sugar.

"Take two," said Dad. "I've got more cooking."

Amelia looked at the tray. The cookies were bright orange with green flecks – another one of Dad's experiments. She grinned at him in relief. How could any dad so dorky be up to anything bad? Well, apart from his cooking, of course. The cookies were bound to be disgusting, but not *evil*.

Overcompensating a bit for her earlier doubts, she bit into a cookie with gusto. To her utter surprise, it was delicious. "Mm, what are they?"

Dad grinned proudly. "Guess!"

Amelia chewed, thoughtfully. "Carrot?"

"Pumpkin and tea leaves!" Dad beamed.

Charlie coughed and spluttered, spraying orange crumbs all over the floor. "These are *healthy*?"

"They're great," said Amelia. "Can I please have another one?"

Dad shoved the cookies at them both, thrilled to have a winner on his hands.

"We saw James," said Amelia, casually. "He said he met Lady Naomi."

"Yeah."

"Did you meet her too? What's she like?"

"Nice," said her dad. "Sweet. Just like my Dr. Walker Pumpkin Tea-Times! Go on, help yourselves. I know you want to."

Amelia grinned and grabbed a handful. "Thanks, Dad."

Charlie made a face. "No thanks, I'm full."

They walked out to the veranda and Charlie's

eyes suddenly lit up. "I nearly forgot – I've got something to show you! Not here, though. C'mon."

He dragged her to the far end of the hotel, rounding a corner and sitting in a little nook seat where they were shielded from view on three sides.

"Check this out." He took from his pocket the little cylinder he'd found the day before, and twisted one of the brass rings. A little light glowed at one end.

"A flashlight?" said Amelia, wondering if they'd finally found something in this place that was *less* mysterious than it seemed.

But then Charlie twisted the ring again, and the light flared up and opened like a little fan. The fan started rotating faster and faster to create a cone of light, its point spinning on the end of the cylinder, its flat end like a circular platform a hand span above.

"Whaaaaaat?" Amelia peered closer, and Charlie twisted the ring a third time.

Now, on the platform of light, a tiny figure appeared – a man wearing an old-fashioned coat that reached past his knees. The figure rotated on the platform so they could see it at all angles.

"Whoa. Charlie. What *is* that?"

"I don't know. This is as far as I got last night before Mum came in and busted me for not sleeping. A spy communicator, maybe?"

Amelia looked at the little figure. Her stomach gave a sudden jolt. If they could see the man in the old coat, did that mean he could see them too?

No, she told herself. The figure on the platform was frozen in place, way too still to be actually alive.

Amelia shook her head. "I don't think it's a real person. More like a 3-D picture of a person. Can it do anything else?"

"I'll try." Charlie twisted a different ring, and a burst of light flashed out of the other end of the cylinder, blinding Amelia for a moment as it blasted straight into her face.

"Whoops! Sorry, Amelia."

She rubbed her face and blinked until her vision came back. "What was that?"

"I don't know, but look – it's shut down now. Or broken."

"Weird."

Charlie shook the cylinder and twisted different rings in various directions and combinations. Nothing happened.

"Hey, your dad's a scientist, right? Have you ever seen anything like this in his stuff?"

"No," said Amelia. "He's not that type of ..."

She trailed off, the weight dropping back into her stomach. She didn't *think* this thing could be anything of Dad's. Or anything Dad would know about. But if he and Mum were keeping secrets for Tom, who knew what *else* they were hiding?

"Do you think he'd be able to figure it out, though?" Charlie pushed.

"No," said Amelia. Then realizing how snappy she'd sounded, she went on, "Actually, James is the one who loves gadgets and puzzles. If you want to ask anyone, you should –"

"It's all right," said Charlie, pulling the cylinder

closer to him. "I'll keep trying on my own for a while."

Amelia looked at the cylinder, her eyes narrowed. There was this thing in science that Dad always talked about: Occam's razor. Only it wasn't really a razor, it was an idea – a principle. It said that whenever you have a problem that needs explaining, the simplest solution is usually the right answer.

Right now, the problem was all over the place: weird, suspect Tom; crazy Miss Ardman; Miss Ardman's foul tank of bugs on one hand and amazing jewels on the other; Mum, Dad and Mary all in on some secret Tom knew about ... and now this funny little cylinder. According to Occam's razor, the right answer should neatly link all those things into one story. But what on earth could link those things together?

"Hey, look," said Charlie. He tried the cylinder

again, and the light came back on.

"Maybe it reset," said Amelia.

Charlie nodded, and twisted the ring so that the little figure of the man appeared. So far, so good. He twisted the same ring a fourth time, and this time the man disappeared but the cone stayed in place. The light kind of blinked as though something was loading, and then – to Amelia's utter shock – she was staring at her own face.

She swallowed hard.

"It's some kind of camera!" Charlie crowed. "It snapped you while you were looking at it. A 3-D digital camera – awesome!"

Amelia shook her head, spooked. Also, she looked kind of terrible – the light image showed her scrunching up her nose and frowning. Was that really what she looked like when she was concentrating?

She turned away in discomfort, but then froze.

She gripped Charlie's arm and whispered, "I heard something."

They listened together, and Charlie heard it too.

Footsteps.

Slow, careful, creaking footsteps coming from inside the hotel. Right behind them.

Amelia looked at the walls and thought. It must be that set of stairs they'd seen Tom go down when they'd caught him in the hotel. And they had to come out somewhere near here.

But who was using them now? And why did they sound so secretive?

Silently, Amelia and Charlie crept along the veranda. The back of the hotel was a ballroom which opened onto a large, low deck and led down to a lawn and gardens. It was also completely screened by tall hedges. Anyone coming out this door would be able to move around the back of the garden almost unseen from any of the hotel's windows.

Anyone, Amelia chided herself. As if she didn't know who it was.

More footsteps, and then a small door opened next to the wide, glass ballroom doors.

It was Tom.

He limped across the deck, down to the garden, through the bushes and then around to the other side of the hotel, in the direction of his own cottage. Amelia saw he was holding a familiar leather bag to his chest. Holding it very tightly, as though cuddling it more than carrying it.

Breathlessly, Amelia and Charlie watched Tom scuttle down the hillside, moving faster than she'd ever seen him move before. Not quite running, but a hurrying, half-skipping urgency, almost as though Tom was ... excited. Amelia thought about how she would feel to have all of those jewels wrapped up in her arms, all warm and golden and close to her heart, and she felt a deep, jealous anger towards Tom.

"That creep," Charlie hissed beside her.

The two of them, without needing to discuss it, had set off across the veranda to follow Tom when another sound gave them pause. Not footsteps this time, but a low, bloodcurdling wail of despair.

And it was coming from right behind them.

CHAPTER EIGHT

Before Amelia and Charlie could move, Miss Ardman charged out of the servants' door and onto the deck. Her head whipped around wildly, trying to see which way the thief had gone, but she was far too nearsighted to notice Amelia and Charlie cowering by the pillar.

Miss Ardman hadn't made another sound. If that had been her upstairs (and who else could it be?), she wasn't wasting any energy on noise now. She gathered up her robes until her legs were bare to the knees, then sniffed the air. Her head snapped around to exactly the direction Tom had taken, and she bolted across the lawn, rushing through the hedges. She was *fast*.

"Come on!" Amelia and Charlie raced after her.

As Amelia and Charlie came through the hedges and ran over the brow of the hill, they saw that Miss Ardman was already right at the bottom of the slope. It was impossible for anyone to be so fast. She had almost caught up to Tom, who was pushing his way through the magnolia trees only a second or two ahead of her.

Amelia pulled ahead of Charlie as they galloped over the lawn. They crashed into the trees, almost a minute after Miss Ardman. They'd never been so far down this end of the grounds, had never wanted to get so close to Tom's cottage, but here they were, crashing through the fallen leaves, snapping twigs, not even caring about making noise. It was clear that Miss Ardman and Tom were far too absorbed in their own chase to notice the two kids tailing them.

As they made it to the clearing around the cottage, they heard an ominous hissing. The door was hanging open, almost torn off its hinges, and Miss Ardman's scarf lay on the step.

After running so far and so fast, Amelia was carried into Tom's cottage partly by sheer momentum, but partly by something else. The jewels. Ever since she and Charlie had first seen them, they'd been tingling away in the back of her brain. And now, running after them, those tinglings had become more urgent.

Any doubts Amelia had about her parents, any guilty fear about upsetting Miss Ardman again, any question about why they were chasing an angry woman who was chasing a creepy man – all of it was swept away by the sheer joy of running towards the beautiful jewels.

Nothing else mattered now.

So there was no hesitation for either Amelia or Charlie as they reached Tom's cottage. Ignoring all the signs of violence at the doorway (were those *slash marks* on the woodwork?), they barreled inside.

Amelia had no idea what she'd expected of Tom's home, but it wasn't this. Charts were pinned up all over the place, like timetables, but in an alphabet Amelia didn't recognize. Dozens of old clocks lay around, and on a desk cluttered by toy trains and empty mugs sat an old computer, wrapped in aluminum foil. Stranger still was the amount of space on one wall given to a contraption that was mostly dials, brass cogs and wire.

Not that Amelia was looking at these things, precisely. They just flashed across her mind as she stared at something even more astounding.

Miss Ardman was *stalking* Tom. There was no other word for it. Her body was hunched and poised like a cat's, ready to pounce. Her hands were held like claws, and Amelia remembered how strong and heavy they could be. She almost felt sorry for Tom, even if he was a lying pirate thief.

Amelia held her breath. Charlie was silent too. They were so close to the jewels – Amelia could swear she felt the warmth of them from here. Amelia looked sideways at Charlie, her eyes huge.

What are we doing here? she asked him silently.

Charlie seemed to know exactly what she meant.

The best thing would be to quietly edge out of the cottage before either Tom or Miss Ardman noticed them. But they stayed where they were. Amelia was frightened, but leaving the jewels would have been unbearable.

Tom and Miss Ardman must surely have known

they were there, but were so focused on one another they'd barely blinked. They were locked in a bizarre sort of standoff that looked as though it could last all night.

Tom's back bumped into the brick wall. Miss Ardman took a step towards him.

And then Tom burst into tears.

Amelia blinked. She hadn't seen that coming.

Tom was now hugging Miss Ardman's case like it was his long lost love, and begging her, "But I need them, I *need* them! Just one?"

Miss Ardman growled deep in her throat – a dark, chilling sound like a crocodile's roar. She stepped closer to Tom and hissed, "Give me the bag."

Tom whimpered. "I – I – I can't."

"You must." Miss Ardman stepped closer again, her hands twitching. She was desperate to snatch back the bag, but at the same time worried about the jewels being broken in the process. "Give it to me," she said more quietly.

Tom took a shuddering breath and raised his head. He looked Miss Ardman straight in the face, and said, shakily and with great effort, "I *can't*. You'll have to. Can you –"

Without warning, Miss Ardman sprang at Tom, hitting him so hard with the back of her hand that he flew across the room and hit the wall, crumpling to the floor. She must have had the reflexes and precision of a ninja brain surgeon, because with no wasted movement, the case was now safely under her arm.

She spun away from Tom so that she was turned more towards Amelia and Charlie, and opened the case to check the jewels were all still there. As the top of the bag opened and shimmering golden light spilled out, Amelia and Charlie both sighed with delight, and began moving closer to them.

Miss Ardman slammed the case shut instantly, and glared down at the kids. "You!"

Amelia cringed, waiting for the blow that would knock her to the wall like Tom, yet still not able to back away from the jewels. But instead, it was Miss Ardman who backed off, one hand holding the case to her, the other reaching out as if to fend off Amelia and Charlie. "No more," she said hoarsely. "Just go. Quickly now, while you still can."

In the corner, Tom groaned and pulled himself upright, holding his head, but focused on the jewels.

Miss Ardman swung around wildly, trying to keep watch on three people in two different places. "Stay down," she hissed at Tom.

And Tom said the last thing Amelia expected.

"I'm sorry."

The tears were gone. This was the Tom Amelia

knew: gruff and surly. "Sorry you had to deal with me like that. I should have been stronger ..."

Miss Ardman shook her head. "Your kind are never strong enough. I thought I warned you about even bringing my food up to my room."

Amelia and Charlie looked at each other in bewilderment, and then Amelia's lip curled in disgust. Miss Ardman couldn't mean the *centipedes*, could she?

"I thought you understood," Miss Ardman went on. "I thought you knew how dangerous it was for you."

Tom shook his head. "I underestimated ..."

"About what?" Charlie blurted out.

Tom looked over at him and glared. "What are you two doing here, anyway? Didn't your parents set you straight about *trespass*?"

"You're mad at us?" Charlie retorted. "We were right about you. You were stealing! And *she* can

prove it – you're a witness," he told Miss Ardman.
"You can tell our parents, and then *you*," he
grinned triumphantly at Tom, "will be fired."

Tom growled in frustration. "Both of you, out
of my house *now*! Or it'll be me talking to your
parents and you getting in trouble."

Amelia set her jaw. "No."

"What?"

"We're not going," Amelia said. "We saw you.
You stole, and we're going to the police, and then
you'll be arrested, and –"

A tremor hit the house, shaking the windows in
their frames and sending several clocks crashing
to the floor.

"What now?" said Charlie.

Amelia stiffened. A harsh wind gusted out
from the far room of Tom's cottage, and the air
was suddenly full of dust and sand.

"I don't have time for this," said Miss Ardman,

and without waiting for an answer, she reached up
to her neck, put her fingers into the flesh of her
throat, and twisted. She pulled out a small object
and dropped it onto
Tom's coffee table.

The instant she
did, Miss Ardman
became a towering,
scaly, sharp-clawed
creature, with wide,
yellow eyes and a
frill of vicious spines
around her
head and
shoulders.
A reptile
monster
in a dress.

CHAPTER NINE

Amelia was amazed she didn't faint, and disappointed not to. Unconsciousness would have been wonderful compared to this – standing face-to-face with ...

She had no words.

No, that wasn't right. She had plenty of words (dinosaur, for instance; nightmare, Godzilla, *please save me*). What she didn't have was any way to make sense of them.

The reptile thing sniffed at Amelia and Charlie, then turned to Tom and said in Miss

Ardman's voice, "They didn't *know*? You let me uncloak in front of *children* and they didn't *know*? What kind of gateway are you running out here?" She shook her head in contempt. "Human clowns. I'll be telling Control about this, I promise you."

She stepped past Amelia and Charlie and shook her head again. "Sorry, children."

Amelia looked at the sharp talons gripping on to the case of jewels, the coarsely folded scaly skin emerging from the sleeves of the robe, and let out a little moan of confusion.

"But," Charlie murmured. "What are you?"

Miss Ardman said more gently, "I'm a –" and she made a clucking, grinding noise in her throat that Amelia couldn't begin to sound out.

Charlie stepped towards her. "But I mean, what *are* you?"

Miss Ardman grinned. "Ah, the big question, not the specific one. I see. Shall I tell them,

Gateway Man?" She flicked her gaze towards Tom. "Shall I spoil your secret and tell them that I'm – what is your charming word for it? An *alien*?"

Charlie gasped and stepped closer again.

Miss Ardman stepped back and held out a warning claw. "No farther."

"Oh, I didn't mean ..."

"Perhaps you don't mean to," she said grimly. "But look at you all!"

It was true. They had all unconsciously crept nearer and nearer to the jewels. She had shrunk away from them until her back was against the wall, and now hissed, "Children or not, I will hit you if you come any closer to me."

"That's nice," said Amelia sarcastically. "It's not as if we were going to –"

"Fall under the spell of my eggs and do everything in your power to steal them from me?" Miss Ardman suggested, her voice bitter, but nervous too.

Amelia jolted. *Eggs?* Those jewels in the case were ...

Miss Ardman saw Amelia's astonished face, and said in a slightly warmer tone, "Yes, these are my unborn children. Perhaps you understand why I was so distraught over them. To you, they are like an addiction, things to crave, but to me ... well, I am their mother. I assume all mothers are the same, whichever galaxy we are from. Wouldn't all mothers fight to protect their children?"

Amelia gulped, and nodded.

The cottage trembled again, and Miss Ardman was abrupt. "I'm going."

She swept past them all, her robes a ripple of color, her tail so heavily spiked that none of them tried to follow the eggs again. She looked back over her shoulder at Tom and said, "Get your house in order, Gateway Man. Control will have an official complaint from me within an hour of my return home."

"Please don't!" Tom said. "Just –"

Miss Ardman turned and stared at him flatly. "Just what?"

Tom was silent.

"Tell me this, then. If you can't even control yourself around aliens, if you can't provide decent security for an ordinary guest –"Amelia goggled to think Miss Ardman might be "ordinary" on any planet "– how would you possibly cope with a visit from a time shifter? Or a band of plague smugglers? Or *Krskn?*"

The floor vibrated threateningly. Amelia's gaze flashed to the floorboards – then over to Charlie, who looked as dazed and overwhelmed as she was – then up at Tom. But before her brain could even formulate a question, Miss Ardman strode on to the back room.

"The front door is over –"Amelia started, but then saw Miss Ardman knew exactly where she was going. Even if it didn't make any sense. She was walking deeper into the cottage, across its bare floorboards, now gritty with sand, and over to a dark shadow in the corner. She stepped into the puddle of gloom, and Amelia saw that it was a hole – no, a set of stone steps, leading down into the ground under Tom's cottage.

"Come here," said Tom urgently. "Now! Away from that room."

They heard Miss Ardman's footsteps growing fainter and more distant, then, as Tom bustled them into the kitchen, the sound of a door being opened and banging closed again. Another great tremor shook the house, and Tom sighed. "She's gone."

Amelia waited to see what might happen next. After a few deep breaths, when it looked as though things might stay normal for at least another five minutes, she turned to Tom.

Tom glared back. "You wretched, nosy, pushy, disobedient –" He seemed too angry to finish what he was going to say, and instead stomped to the sink and filled the kettle.

"Well?" Charlie demanded, his hands on his hips.

"What?" Tom kept his back to them both.

Amelia snorted. "Erm, let's see ..." She pretended to think hard. "How about: eggs that make you crazy drunk just to look at them, people looking like people but really being aliens, aliens living under your house, and you getting busted because you can't cope with someone called Kristen?"

"Krskn," said Tom, flinching.

"What?"

"The person I can't cope with," said Tom more clearly, "is called Krskn. Also," he smiled slightly, "there are no aliens living under my house."

"But," Charlie began.

Tom held up a weary hand. The half-mangled one, but Amelia was by now so far beyond missing fingers, she didn't notice.

"Let's get it all over with at once," he said. "I'll take you back up to the hotel and let your parents explain it all to you."

Amelia staggered. It was the final blow. After all the impossible, unbelievable things she'd just had crammed into her head, this was the worst. All her doubts had been confirmed.

"My *parents* know about this?"

CHAPTER TEN

Everyone was in the staff room for Tom's emergency meeting. Mum and Dad sitting rather rigidly together, Mary looking almost despairing, and Tom ...

Amelia couldn't erase the image of Tom blubbering over Miss Ardman's eggs. She'd thought there was nothing more uncomfortable than seeing an adult angry and threatening like Miss Ardman, but it had been excruciating to see one helpless and pitiful like Tom.

Tom didn't seem too happy about being seen

like that either. He'd avoided eye contact with any of them for the whole meeting, and had been twice as grumpy as usual.

James wasn't sitting at the table with the rest of them. There was an old chest freezer along one wall of the staff room and he was sitting on that, a disbelieving sneer on his face.

"Aliens?" he snorted. "Really?"

Dad smiled broadly. "Isn't it incredible?"

"Oh, yeah," said James with mock enthusiasm. "Totally! As in: totally *not* credible. As in: a great big pile of bull."

Dad frowned, puzzled. "But you heard what Amelia and Charlie said. You heard Tom backing them up. Why would we say any of that unless –"

James held up a hand. "I have no idea. I mean, obviously, dragging us all out here to this dead-end loser town, you must be trying to destroy our lives. Maybe trying to derange us with made-up stories is part of that. Maybe we're all part of a new experiment of yours now?"

"Hey, Jamo," said Dad. "Hang on now –"

But James had already hopped off the freezer and stalked out of the room. "Not interested," he called back.

Dad got up to go after him, but Mum caught his hand. "No, leave him, Scott. Let him have some time to think it through by himself."

Dad sighed and shook his head. "Not exactly what I was expecting from him."

"Expecting, Scott? But you weren't *expecting* the kids to find anything out, right?" said Mum. "That was the deal, wasn't it? We keep them separate from it for as long as possible?"

"Yeah, well." Dad glanced bashfully at Tom. "Top secret. But I thought that if they ever did find out, they'd think it was, you know ..."

"Totally awesome!" Charlie finished for him.

Dad grinned. "Exactly."

Mary shook her head and looked anxiously at her son. "Charlie, do you understand just how important it is to keep this quiet? We all know the truth now, but you can't tell anyone else about what you've seen. *No one*. Not even in hints, or as a joke, or pretending it's a make-believe game. No one can know anything about Miss Ardman or what goes on in Tom's cottage."

"But what *does* go on there?" Charlie interrupted her. "Miss Ardman has gone, but gone where?"

Dad looked even more excited and leaned in to speak. Mum laid a hand on his arm again.

"Are you sure, Scott?" she said. "Once you tell them, you can't take it back. What if Control ...?"

Dad shrugged. "Miss Ardman's complaint is more than enough to bring Control down on us, and the kids already know the main points. All I'm going to do is fill in the ... mechanics a little.

Better they understand properly from us than try to figure it out on their own, don't you think?"

Mum looked at Amelia and Charlie, and then over at Mary. The two mothers sighed at each other, and Dad took that as agreement. He grinned.

"Now, Amelia, you know that my research has been into the possibility of the existence of worm-holes – giant deformities that could theoretically join two distant points in space together?"

Amelia nodded.

"So ..." Dad coaxed her. "What do you think could be in the caves under Tom's house?"

"A wormhole," Amelia breathed.

"No!" Dad crowed. "Not *a* wormhole – hundreds of them! Perhaps thousands! A whole spaghetti bowl of wormholes, all shifting and jostling each other, taking it in turns to line up with the gateway under Tom's house."

Amelia gazed at him, trying to fathom it.

"Isn't it amazing?" Dad gushed. "All my life, I've been trying just to prove that the math works, never even hoping to find a single shred of physical evidence, and now – forget evidence! Any time I want, I can go down to Tom's and actually *hear* the wormholes come and go. I can *smell* the air of other planets in other galaxies ..."

Tom grunted and stared at his hands. He didn't seem to share Dad's wonder. Amelia suspected that living on top of all those wormholes might have turned out to be less fun for Tom than Dad supposed.

"So," Charlie grinned at Amelia's dad. "Miss Ardman wasn't a one-off? There will be other aliens coming to stay here?"

"Yeah," said Dad. "From all over. Turns out," he said proudly, "that we have the most active wormhole hub in the whole Milky Way! Can you believe it? In Forgotten Bay!"

"But," Mum broke in, "we're going to have some

human guests too. They're bound to show up once we open for business – and we can't very well turn them away without raising suspicion."

"But," said Amelia, "the … uh … gateway hasn't just opened, has it? Hasn't Tom been looking after it all this time? So what's changed? What are we here for?"

Tom grunted again. This time it sounded like he approved of Amelia's questions.

Mum looked pained. "Everything's changed. Tom's handled this whole place on his own for years, and he's done brilliantly," she added. Tom sniffed, but turned pink. "But things are different now."

"How?"

"The wormholes are becoming more unpredictable for one thing," said Dad. "It could be something to do with the natural acceleration of the expansion of the universe, or it could be a new instability –" He stopped, realizing he'd lost Amelia. "Well, to put it simply, Tom's old charts and timetables are getting less and less useful in predicting when the wormholes will arrive, and the wormhole connections themselves are getting less reliable. So there's a lot of work here for me just on the physics."

"And," said Mum, "Gateway Control–who oversee and regulate all the gateways in use – are getting nervous about letting this gateway stay in our hands. They'd much rather have their own people running it, and we're kind of on probation to see if we're up to the job. Miss Ardman's complaint isn't going to help."

"But that would never work," said Charlie. "If aliens are supposed to be a big secret, how could they run it?"

"You saw Miss Ardman," said Dad. "Did she look like an alien?"

Amelia shuddered. "I'll say!"

"No, I mean when you first met her. She looked human, didn't she? All our alien guests – and any

Gateway Control officials who come here to check on us – will all be cloaked by holo-emitters. Tom, do you have one to show them?"

Tom scowled more deeply still. "Nope."

"Ah, well," Dad went on. "They're amazing, basically clockwork with a crystal core. They're these tube things that you stick on your neck ..."

Amelia and Charlie looked at each other in startled recognition. Charlie swallowed a grin.

"... and you not only look like another person, you are physically wearing that form, too. I mean, you could have touched Miss Ardman and felt human skin, not scales. It's brilliant."

"It's dangerous," Tom spoke up.

"Tom," Mum started.

But Tom retorted angrily. "No. If you want them to know the truth, then they should know the whole truth. The gateway is *dangerous*. Not just because it's speeding up or unstable.

Not just because Control want to interfere. It's dangerous because we are standing in the middle of an intergalactic superhighway – just standing in the middle of the traffic, totally unprotected, and *hoping* that we don't get hit by anything."

"Tom," Mum said warningly. "Don't frighten –"

"No, I *will* frighten them," said Tom. "I *want* them frightened. Because frightened kids might take things seriously, and stay as far away from the gateway as possible. Frightened kids will have, maybe, a two percent advantage, and if ever Krskn –"

"Right!" Dad said loudly, standing up and clapping his hands together. "Right! Good point, Tom, thank you! OK, great meeting, everyone. Now off you go, kids!"

"But –" said Amelia.

"Ba-ba-ba!" Dad said over the top of her, refusing to listen. "Out you go! Now!"

Amelia didn't push it. The moment Tom had

said "Krskn," all the hair stood up on the back of her neck. She had no idea why, but she didn't want to hear any more about what went on in those caves under Tom's cottage.

"Charlie," Mary called after them. "It's all secret, remember?"

"Yes, Mum," Charlie groaned.

"I mean it, Charlie. For the first time, I really, literally mean it when I say you could get yourself in worlds of trouble."

Charlie made a face at Amelia, and they went out through the lobby into the bright innocent sunshine. Over at the edge of the headland, James was throwing rocks out at the ocean below. She decided not to walk that way.

"Come on, Charlie," she said. "We never checked out whether that really is a hedge maze."

"Yeah!" said Charlie.

They broke into a run, and Amelia grinned,

wondering if maybe life here could be almost normal. Maybe it wasn't going to be all drama and mystery. Mum and Dad were still on her side – and surely they could handle whatever else decided to drop into Tom's cottage. Meanwhile, Amelia had Charlie for company, and she could play on the beach, and she was going to get that puppy soon.

Behind her, she heard Charlie call out, "And when we get right into the middle of the maze, I'm going to get back to work on this holo-emitter in my pocket!"

OK, so maybe "almost normal" was pushing it. Maybe, in fact, life at the Gateway Hotel was going to turn out to be pretty much the opposite of normal. Perhaps even dangerous at times.

Somehow, though, with Charlie beside her and the whole headland bathed in golden afternoon light while the waves crashed endlessly below, Amelia couldn't help feeling excited.

Cerberus Jones

Cerberus Jones is the three-headed writing team made up of Chris Morphew, Rowan McAuley and David Harding.

Chris Morphew is *The Gateway's* story architect. Chris's experience writing adventures for *Zac Power* and heart-stopping twists for *The Phoenix Files* makes him the perfect man for the job!

Rowan McAuley is the team's chief writer. Before joining Cerberus Jones, Rowan wrote some of the most memorable stories and characters in the best-selling *Go Girl!* series.

David Harding's job is editing and continuity. He is also the man behind *Robert Irwin's Dinosaur Hunter* series, as well as several *RSPCA Animal Tales* titles.